Ice
Cat

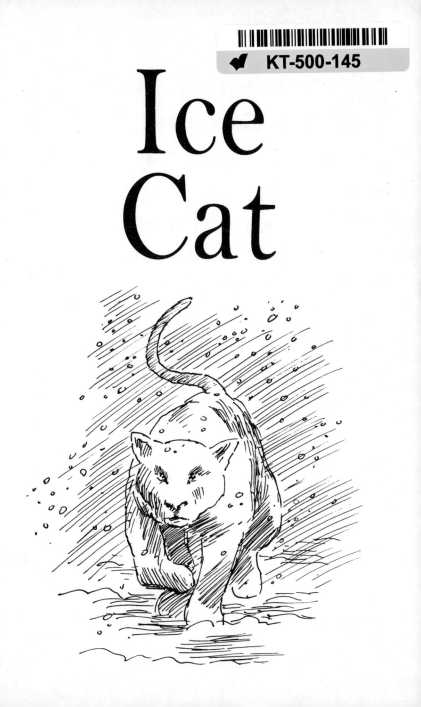

Also by Linda Newbery
The Marmalade Pony
Smoke Cat

For older readers
The Nowhere Girl
Flightsend

Ice
Cat

Linda Newbery

Illustrated by
Peter Kavanagh

SCHOLASTIC
PRESS

For Linda and Andy – another cat.
L.N.
For Mary, with love from Pete.
P.K.

Scholastic Children's Books,
Commonwealth House,
1–19 New Oxford Street,
London WC1A 1NU, UK
a division of Scholastic Ltd
London ~ New York ~ Toronto ~ Sydney ~ Auckland
Mexico City ~ New Delhi ~ Hong Kong

First published in the UK by Scholastic Ltd, 1997
This edition, 1999

Text copyright © Linda Newbery, 1997
Illustrations © Peter Kavanagh, 1997

ISBN 0 439 01171 X

Typeset by DP Photosetting, Aylesbury, Bucks.
Printed by Cox & Wyman Ltd, Reading, Berks.

2 4 6 8 10 9 7 5 3 1

The rights of Linda Newbery and Peter Kavanagh to be identified respectively as the
author and illustrator of this work has been asserted by them in accordance with the
Copyright, Designs and Patents Act, 1988.

Chapter One

It was the best snowfall Tom had seen for years. Sometimes, there had been a dusty sprinkling that melted into the roads and made them black and shiny. Sometimes there was a thick frost overnight that left a white fur on trees and walls and car windscreens. Sometimes there were curly patterns on the window, like ferns, that faded away when Tom breathed on them. But never before had he seen so much clean, sparkling, new, *deep* snow, that made

him want to run in it and roll in it and scoop
it up and throw it.

He went out in front of the house to
look. Still the flakes came down, big and
soft, as if someone had emptied out a huge
sack of feathers and shaken them free.

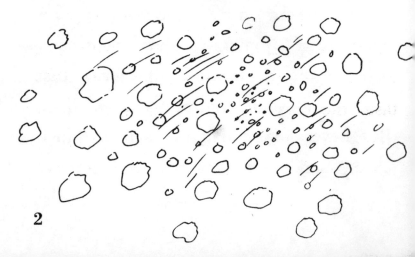

Tom felt dizzy when he looked up at the sky
and saw the white feathery flakes whirling.
He could catch them on his tongue and
taste the crystal coldness of them. The
tracks his feet made filled quickly with soft
new snow.

Next door, Gary and his dad were getting ready to come out, pulling on their wellingtons in the porch. "We're going to build a snowman!" Gary shouted, leaping out, landing splat, then staggering forward, leaving two deep footmarks where he'd stood. "You can help if you want."

Gary's dad came out too, in a red fleece jacket and bobble hat. The small front garden was shared by the two houses. There was no fence between and usually the front garden was just a thin strip of green – usually. Now, it was a strip of white, dazzling and untouched, like a fresh page that made you want to write on it. Gary's dad had shovelled and swept the snow away from the path to their front door, but Tom's front path was still as the snowfall had left it, with two sets of footprints up to the door and back, left by the milkman and the postman.

"No, thanks. I'm going to build my own," Tom shouted back.

If Gary's dad hadn't been there, Tom would have said yes straight away. It would have been fun to build a snowman with Gary. But it was different with Gary's dad there.

He went back indoors for his gloves, and to tell Mum he was staying outside. When he came back out, they'd already started, Gary and his dad: rolling a ball of snow that was getting bigger and bigger.

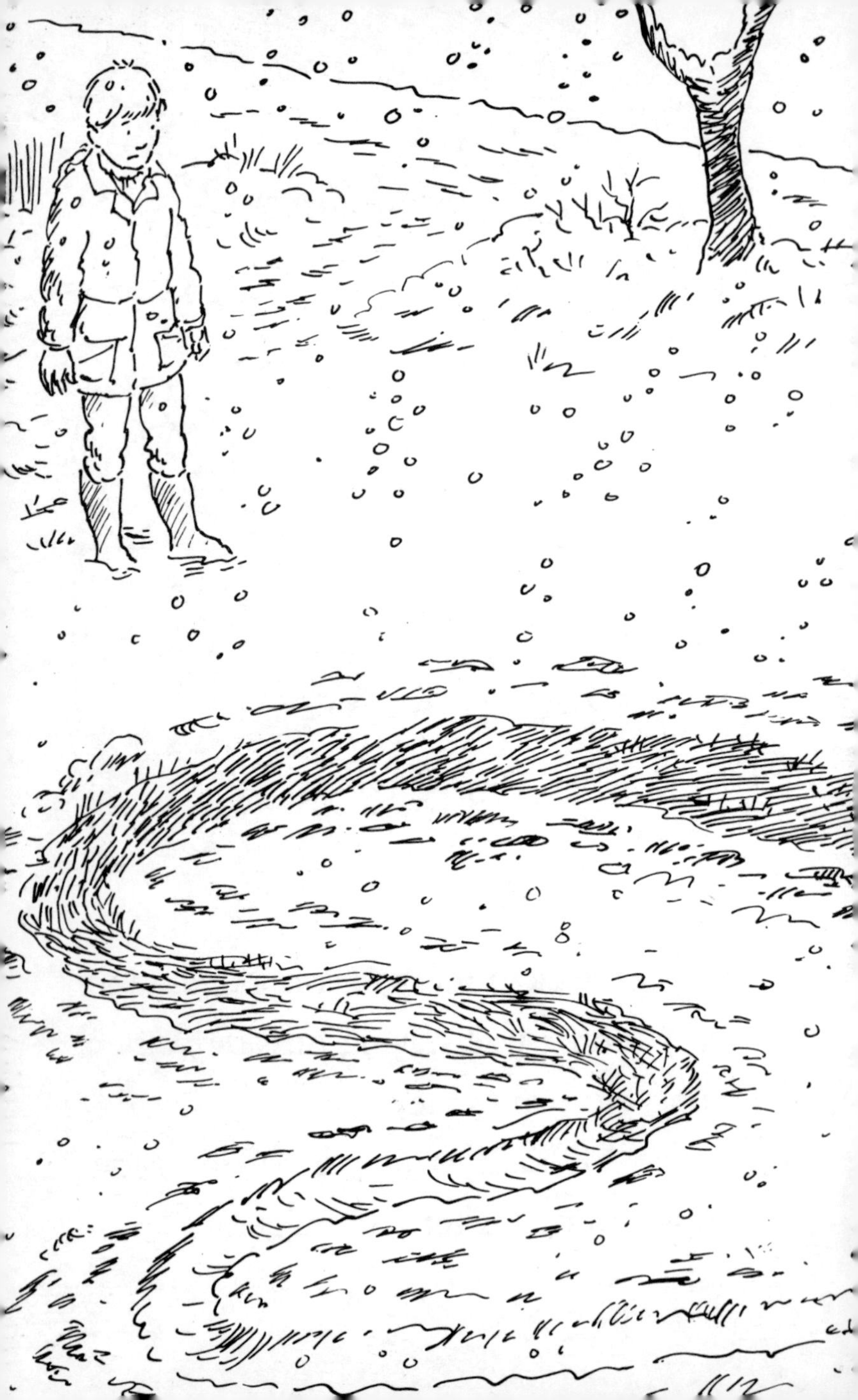

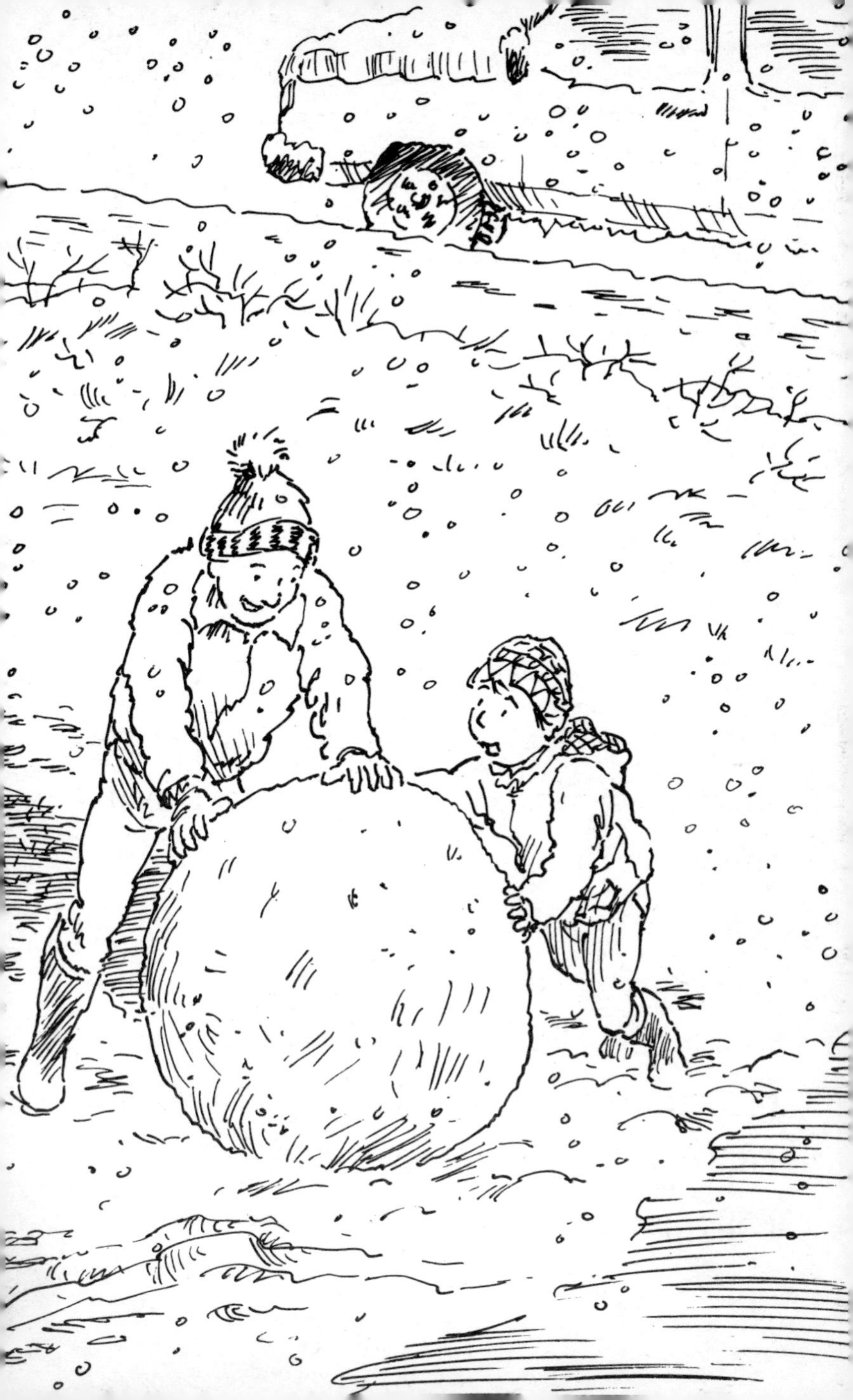

They were spoiling the snow, making a big flattened track round their part of the garden. They kept to their own half, as if there were a rule about it. Tom had the feeling that they were making it a competition. And because Gary's dad was there, he wanted to win. He had to make a better snowman than theirs.

He didn't want to copy, so instead of rolling a big snowball for the body he collected snow in his hands, scooping it up, piling it into a heap, shaping and patting it. *His* snowman was going to be different. Different and better.

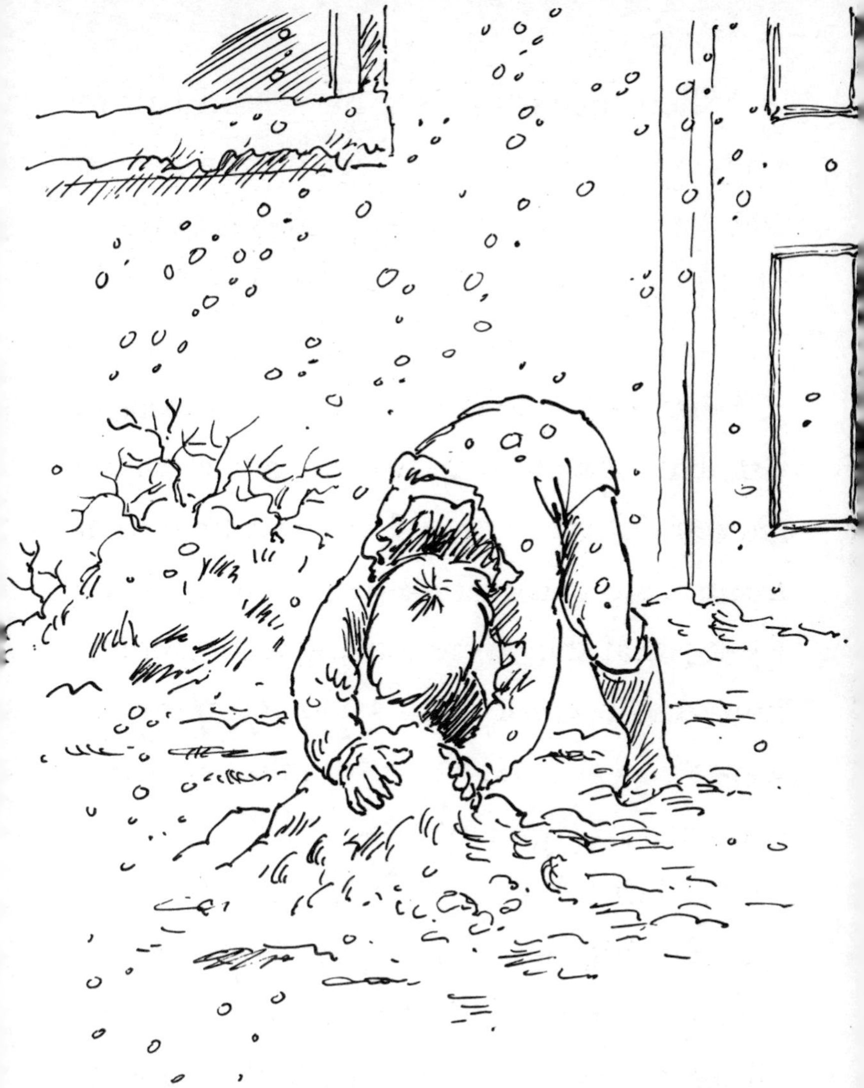

When they'd made a big round ball for the body, Gary and his dad rolled a second, smaller ball for the head, and set it on top. Theirs was already looking like a jolly snowman, the sort Tom had seen on Christmas cards. A fat, jolly, round-faced snowman, who would soon have a smiling face and a carrot nose. He would be big and round and cheerful like Gary's dad.

Tom's own snowman wasn't at all like that. As he added more snow, and patted and smoothed and moulded it, the snow figure was taking a shape of its own. He could feel it through his soaking gloves, a firm, growing shape. It would only grow the way it wanted. If he tried to add bits that weren't right, the snow crumbled and slid off.

The shape refused to become a snow-man. It felt to Tom as if there was a creature inside the snow, pushing its way out. It didn't want to stand upright, but crouched on the ground, a firm, huddled, living shape.

At last he stepped back and looked at it and saw what it was.

Chapter Two

Gary aimed a snowball. "That's a funny-looking snowman! Couldn't you get it to stand up? Ours does!"

The snowball spattered on the back of Tom's anorak and a few wet bits slithered down his neck, but he took no notice. He could get Gary back later.

"It's not meant to be standing up," he said. "Anyone can make a snowman. Mine's different. Mine's a snow *cat*."

Gary's dad came closer to look. "Yes, I

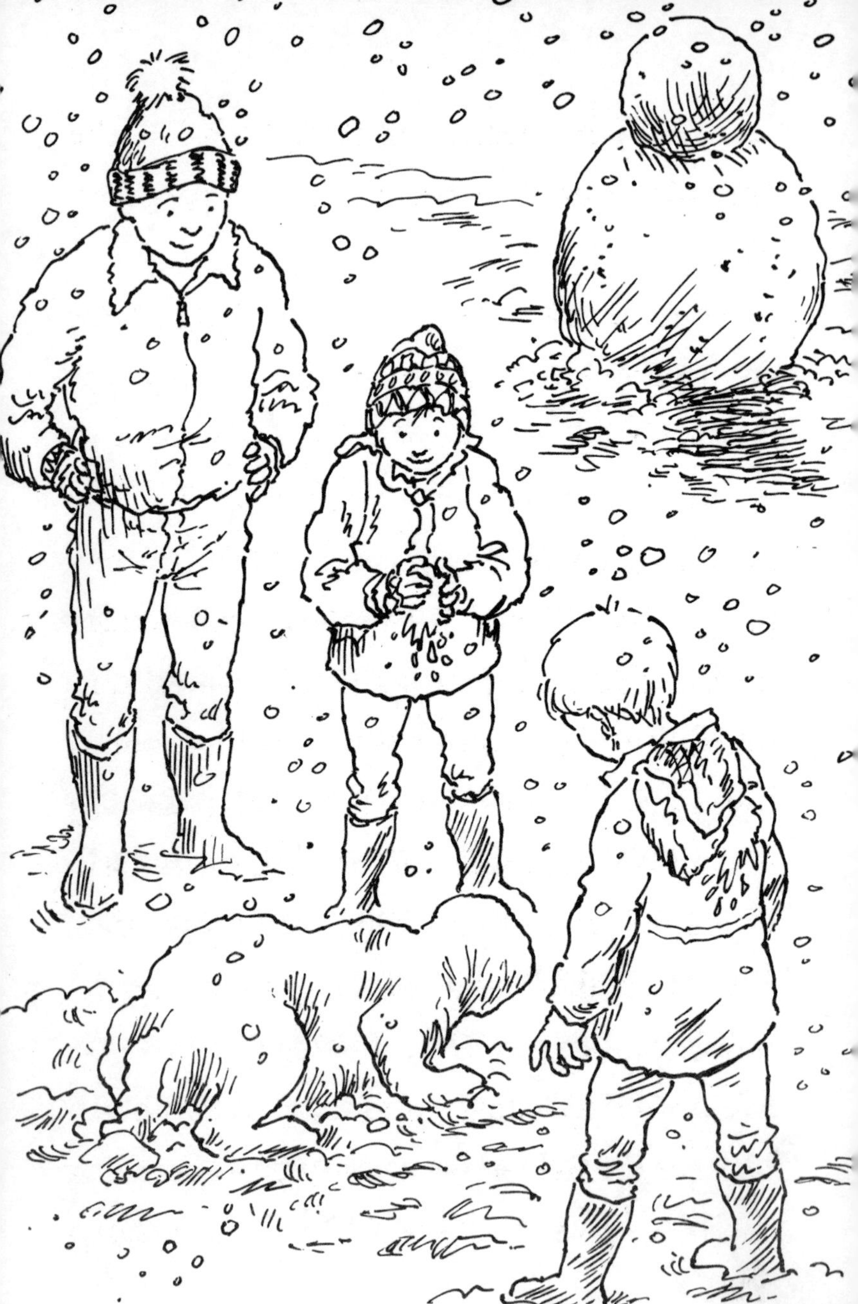

see what you mean," he said. "It's like the animals your dad makes. It's very good, Tom."

Tom didn't want anyone looking at his snow cat until it was finished. And anyway, he didn't know if Gary's dad *really* liked it, or if he was just trying to be kind, because he thought Tom hadn't been able to make a proper snowman. The snow cat wasn't anything like as good as Dad's carved animals; but Tom didn't want to think about those. He ignored Gary's dad and carried on working. He scooped up more snow and modelled its ears, the dip at the back of its neck, and then added a long sweep for its tail. It crouched there, waiting.

Gary's dad went in and fetched two black buttons for the snowman's eyes, a carrot for the nose, and a strip of liquorice to make a wide smiling mouth, and he tied his own scarf round its neck. Then he took off his bobble hat and put it on the snowman's head. Gary's mum came out to look, and then she went back indoors for her camera and took two photographs of it. She had to use the flash, because it was already starting to get dark.

"Take one of Tom's as well," Gary's dad said, pointing. "He's made a cat, look."

"No," Tom said quickly. "It's not finished yet."

The snow cat, he could tell somehow, didn't want to be photographed. It wasn't like the smiling Christmas-card snowman.

Gary and his mum and dad went indoors, and Tom completed his work on the snow cat, modelling the face and the ears, tracing in a nose, eyes, curved mouth and whiskers.

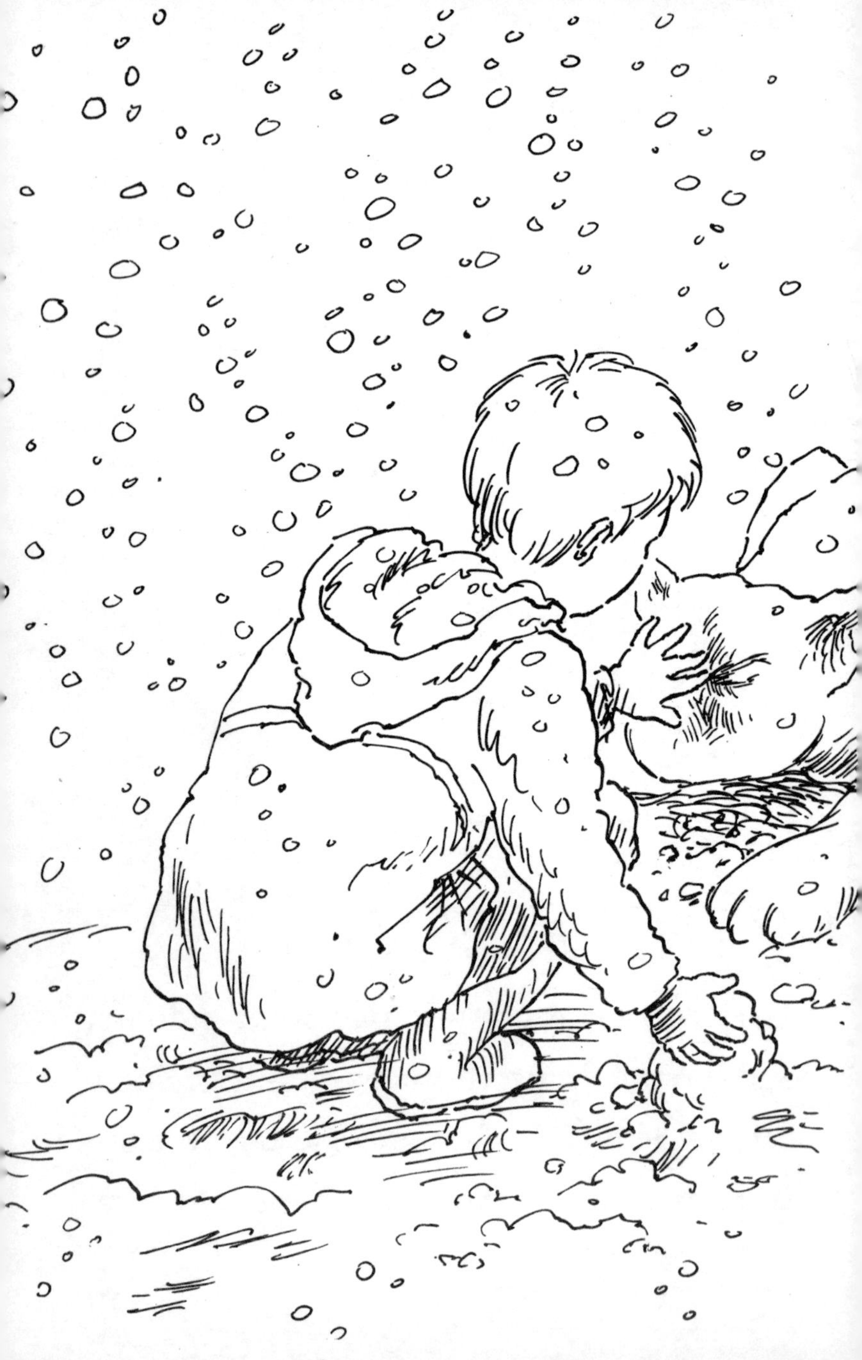

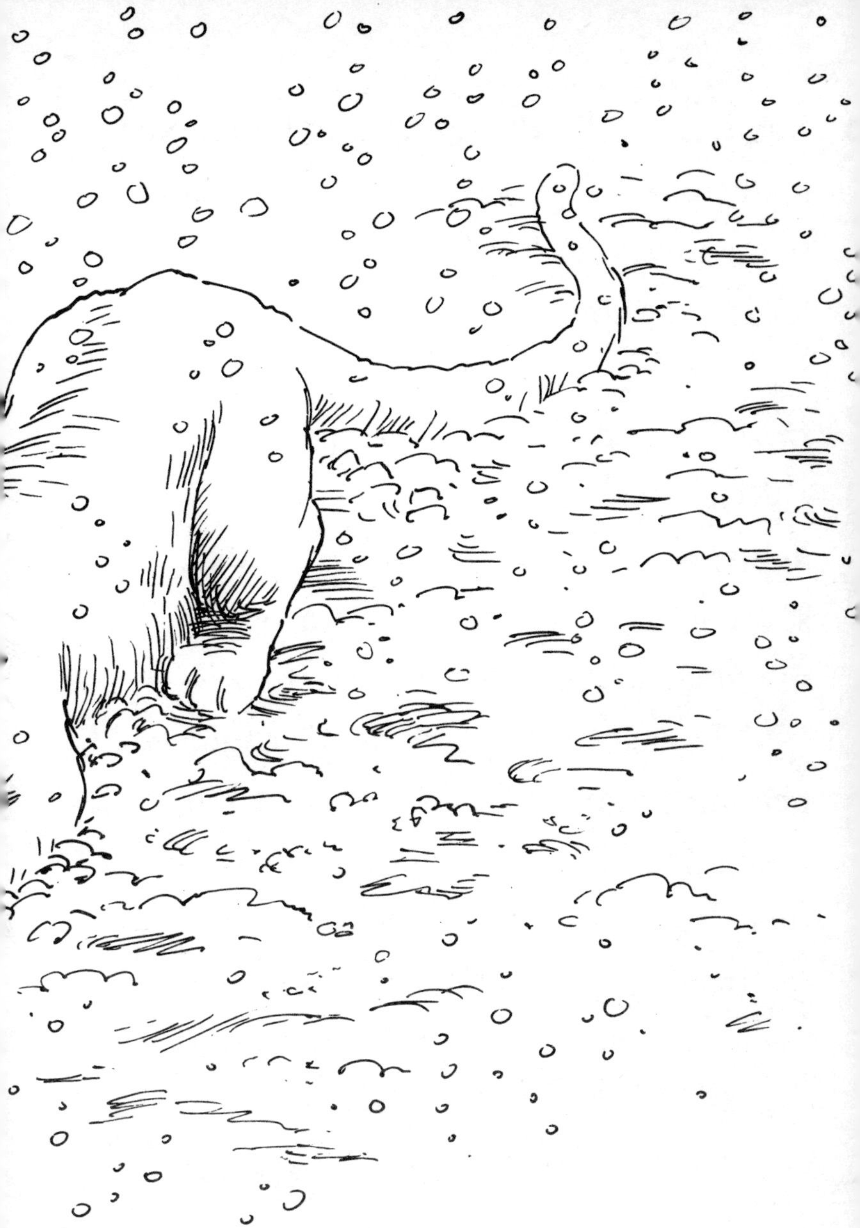

Suddenly it didn't feel right to be touching it any more. The eyes were only scratches in the snow face, but they seemed to be looking at him.

"Tommy, come on! Aren't you getting frozen out there?"

Mum was at the door, shivering. The lights were on in the house, making the snow look blue and icy. Tom noticed for the first time how very cold it was.

"That's a funny snowman," Mum said, peering from the doorstep. "For a minute I thought it was some wild animal crouching there."

"It's a snow cat," Tom said. "I didn't mean it to be but it just sort of turned into one."

It was a relief to go indoors, to stamp the snow off his boots, to take off his anorak and his soaking gloves. The TV was on but there was no sign of Dad.

"He's still not well enough to come down," Mum said, guessing what Tom was thinking as he looked at Dad's empty chair. "Why don't you go up and tell him about your snowman – I mean snow cat? That'd cheer him up. And ask him if he wants anything taken up."

It wouldn't cheer Tom up, but he went anyway, walking upstairs as slowly as he could. Dad was sitting up in bed, reading.

He looked thin and tired, but he smiled at Tom and said, "Did you have fun? Mum said you were making a snowman with Gary. I bet it's a good one."

"I made it by myself," Tom said. "And it's not a snowman, it's a cat."

He could hear the way his voice sounded, bad-tempered and sulky. There was something about seeing Dad propped up against the pillows, thin and frail, that made Tom feel moody. Dad shouldn't *be* like that. Dad hadn't always been ill: and dads were supposed to be like Gary's dad – big and loud and strong and boisterous, dressed in red jackets and bobble hats, full of energy enough to make the biggest and best snowman ever. It wasn't *fair*.

"I'd love to see it," Dad said, looking at the window. "But it's too dark now. First thing in the morning."

"It might not be there by morning," Tom said.

He knew it would be – all that snow wasn't going to melt in one night – but he felt like saying it, and anyway Dad might not be well enough to get out of bed. Dad looked as if he might never get out again. The blankets seemed to crush him and the

book he was holding looked too heavy for his hands. Those hands had made dozens of carved animals, the horses and elephants and squirrels that sprang to life out of lumps of soapstone. But Dad hadn't carved any animals for months now, since his hands had become knotted and painful. Tom hated to look at Dad's hands now.

Tom went to the window and pushed the curtains aside to look out. The pane of glass was cold on his forehead and his breath made a steamy, damp cloud against his reflection. He felt as if he had swallowed a big lump of ice. He could feel it inside him, a cold hard lump that wouldn't melt.

Outside, the street lamps made pools of warmth on the snowy pavement. Tom leaned closer to look straight down into the front garden and saw the snow cat,

crouching, as if it would spring. It was an ice cat now, cold and blue, lurking in the shadow of the house. Tom was surprised to see what a good job he had made of it, after all. It looked like a real cat, curled ready to pounce, as if it would leap forward the moment he closed the curtain and stopped watching it. He felt proud to have made it, and he knew Dad would love to see it too. But what he felt wasn't a warming glow of pride – it was more like the lump of ice inside him growing bigger and colder, because he'd made something on his own, something full of life and energy. As if he'd done it to get his own back at Dad.

"Do you want anything?" he asked Dad sulkily, because Mum had asked him to.

"No, thanks," Dad said. "It'll be teatime soon."

30

Downstairs in the kitchen, Tom said to Mum, "He isn't going to get better, is he?"

Mum was making toast at the grill. She leaned down to hug Tom with one arm and he pulled a face because he knew that meant she was going to say something bad.

31

"No, Tommy, he isn't. Sometimes he'll be a bit better and sometimes he'll be worse. The pills help. But he'll never be completely well again. We'll all have to get used to it."

Chapter Three

That night, when Tom was ready for bed, he went to the window and looked out. His feet were cold, and he felt a cold draught rush at him from the window, but he wanted to see the ice cat again.

It took a few moments for his eyes to adjust to the darkness. When they did, he looked at the place where the ice cat should have been. There was no cat, nothing, not even a crumpled heap of snow. Just a flattened patch where it had been crouching.

Tom shivered. He looked towards his bookshelf, where there were three of Dad's carved animals: an elephant, a horse and a tall thin bird on stilty legs. In the shadows, even they looked as if they might behave strangely – the elephant's trunk looked poised to lift, the horse was about to rear up and strike out its forelegs, and the stilty bird looked as if it might stretch its wings and fly across the bedroom, towards Tom. He got into bed and pulled the quilt up to his ears.

He fell asleep quickly, but woke again in the middle of the night and then lay awake for a long time. He couldn't stop thinking about that flattened patch of snow where the ice cat had been. But the ice cat couldn't *move*. He must have imagined it, or been dreaming.

The night was so still and quiet that he couldn't hear a sound. Not a mumble or a snore from Mum and Dad's room; not a car passing on the road outside. Only the creak of his bed, too loud, when he turned over. He knew he wouldn't be able to sleep until he got out of bed and looked out of the window, just a quick look. . .

The central heating had gone off hours ago and the air was like an icy blanket wrapping itself round him as he got out of bed. He went to the window and felt the cold air burning his face. He looked out, trying not to breathe too hard and steam up the glass.

There was just the palest glimmer of blue light on the snow, the first light of dawn. Everything was quiet and still, frozen in sleep.

And underneath the window was the flattened patch of snow, just as he had seen it before. He *hadn't* imagined it. The ice cat hadn't crumbled away or melted – the night was too cold for that. It was on the move, leaving the snow crushed and trodden where it had lain, like a real cat would. He knew that if he took a torch outside and looked, he'd be able to see claw-marks in the snow.

And then he saw it. Like a shadow that had come to life. Moving slowly along the fronts of the houses, lifting its paws with a cat's slow delicacy. A long, sleek ice cat with eyes that burned into the snow. It moved out of sight around the corner, as if it was circling the row of houses. It was prowling, stalking, searching: Tom didn't know what it was searching for but he could tell it wanted *something*.

He shivered and scrambled back into bed and pulled the quilt right over his head. But he couldn't shut out the ice cat. He had made it and now it was on the move. He imagined it out there, prowling, stalking, its glittery eyes looking for him.

And no matter how much he curled himself up in his duvet and tried to think about something else, the ice cat was there, outside. And inside him as well. It had breathed its spell into the house and trapped him. Its icy breath was a chilly cloud that spread inside his rib-cage and shivered through his arms and legs.

It was the longest night Tom could ever remember. He didn't know whether he was awake or asleep, dreaming of the ice cat's claws scratching at the window, its green eyes glaring through the glass. Glaring at him.

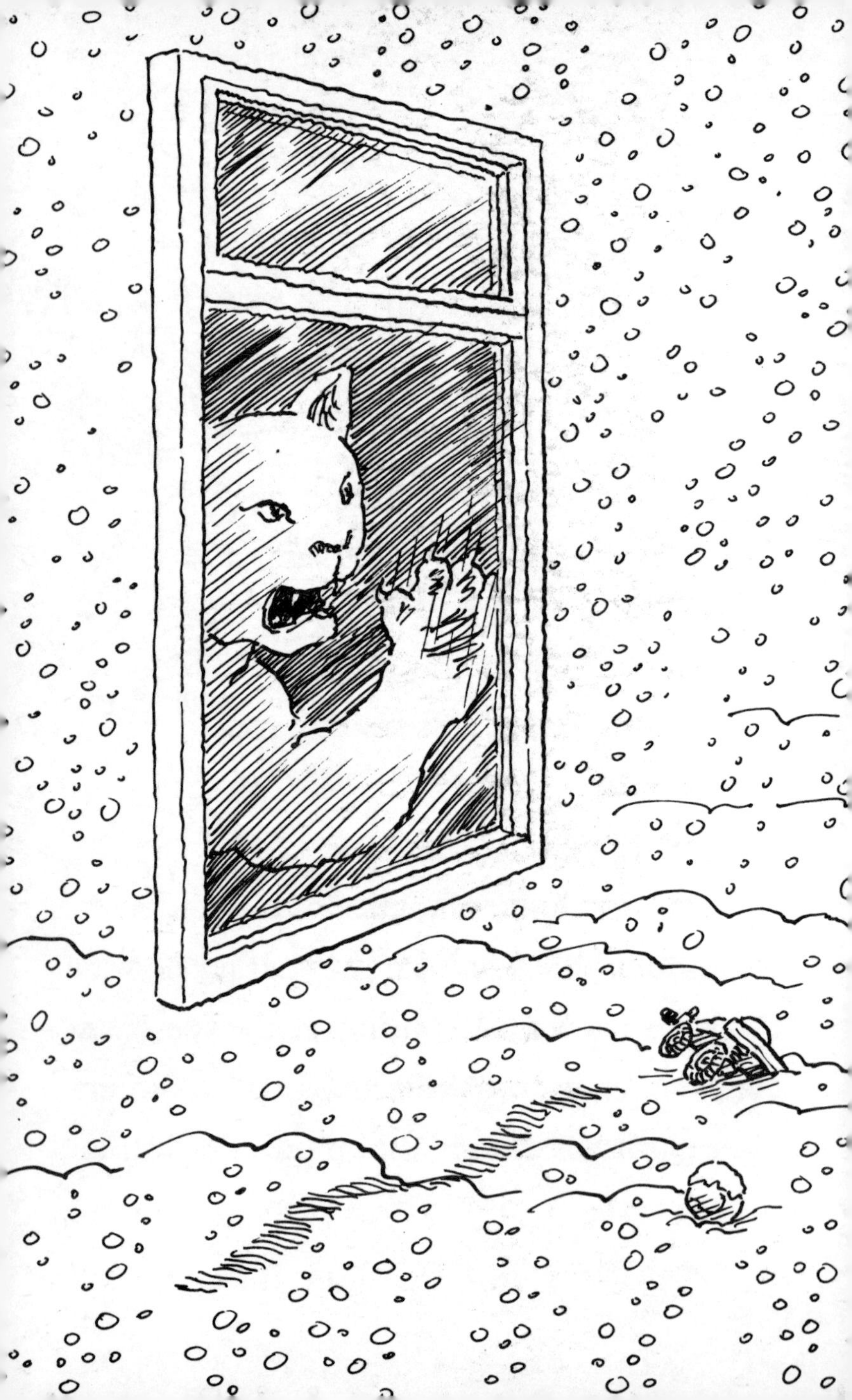

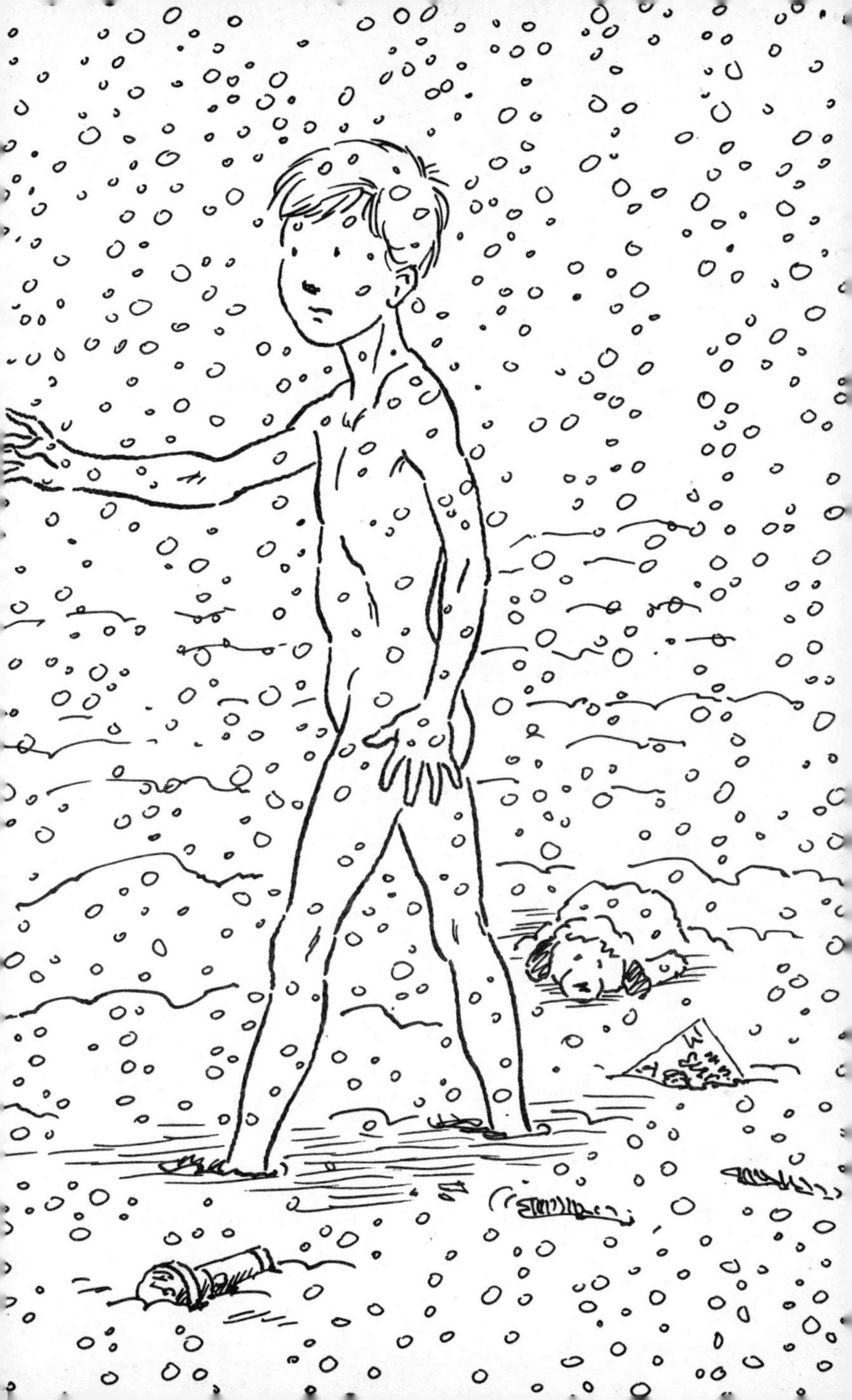

Chapter Four

In the morning, the ice cat was back in its place in the front garden, crouching. It was pretending to be a harmless snow cat, and its eyes were just scratches on its face, not at all glittery or angry. Anyone who didn't know would have thought it was just a snow cat, a snow figure that would soon shrink and melt. But Tom could still feel its icy touch inside him, as if part of the night wouldn't go away.

Mum and Dad were still in bed. Tom put

on his coat and boots and went out into the garden. He didn't know what he was going to do, but he walked to the cat and put a hand on its head and felt the icy touch of it burn through his glove. It was still alive.

And then, as if the cat had told him to, he crossed to Gary's garden where the snow-man stood with a big smug liquorice grin on its face.

"You won't grin any more!" Tom said to it. He aimed a great kick, and his boot gouged into the snowman's side. Then he pushed the round head until it plopped off into the snow and lay there, half sunk. Now

he wouldn't have to look at its horrible grinning face any more. He didn't know what was making him so angry. He felt like a can of fizzy drink that had been shaken up and then opened, so that all the fizziness exploded into his arms and legs and head. He had to let it out somehow. He kicked and stamped and trod and punched until the snowman was a footmarked heap on the ground.

The button eyes and carrot nose and liquorice mouth were nowhere to be seen, the bobble hat was buried somewhere and the scarf trailed limply, encrusted with ice. Tom jumped on top of the heap, in victory. He'd done it! He'd beaten the snowman.

"*Tom!* What are you doing?"

It was Mum's voice, from the upstairs window. She sounded horrified. Tom looked up at her and then down at the trampled remains of the snowman, and his fizzy feeling died away, all the bubbles going flat. What had he done? What would Gary say? What would Gary's dad say? Their curtains were still closed and for a second he thought of trying to rebuild the snowman before any of them noticed. Or he could just run away and pretend someone else had done it. But now Mum knew, and she would be angry. Of course she'd be angry. You couldn't expect to go into other people's gardens and kick their snowmen to pieces and get away with it. Gary and his dad would be even angrier.

"It's all your fault!"

He ran across to the ice cat, and stamped and kicked until it too was just a pile of trodden snow. His heart was thumping and he felt as if he was burning up inside. He ran indoors, kicked off his boots and anorak and hurtled upstairs to his own room. Mum tried to stop him on the landing, but he pushed past her and slammed his bedroom door.

"Tom? What's wrong?" He could hear her voice, puzzled and upset, but he wouldn't answer. He flung himself down on his bed and buried his face, pulling the pillow up to muffle his ears.

Mum came in, and Tom could tell that she didn't know whether to be worried, or cross, or both at once.

"Tom? What's wrong? Why have you spoiled Gary's snowman?"

"I don't know," Tom mumbled.

"What do you mean, you don't know? How can you not know? What did you do it for? You must have had a reason. Come on, Tom, tell me."

Tom could only shake his head, not looking at her. He didn't have a reason.

He could hear Dad coming into the room, walking slowly and carefully, his stick thumping on the floor. Tom didn't look up. He hated to see Dad walking with a stick, as if he was old.

"Let me talk to him," Dad said quietly to Mum.

"Well, all right," Mum said. "If you think you can get any sense out of him."

Mum went away, and Dad sat down carefully on the edge of the bed and laid his stick on the floor. He said nothing at all for a few minutes, and then he took something out of his pocket and turned it over in his hands. Tom couldn't see what it was.

"I haven't made any animals for a while," Dad said, almost as if he was talking to himself. "But this is the last one I made. Just after I found out how ill I was."

"Let me see," Tom said, sitting up.

Dad handed him a small carving. It was made of green soapstone, marbled with white, like green ice. It was a cat – a fierce, arch-backed, spitting cat – with a face screwed up tight with anger. Its eyes glared, cold and green.

Their glare was like sharp splinters of ice, that pierced through Tom and reached the cold heavy lump inside him.

"I didn't mean it to turn out like that,"
Dad said, holding it in his palm. "It seemed
to come out of the stone, as if it was already
there. An angry cat, waiting. I don't like it
much. That's why I haven't put it out with
the other carvings. But I'm still going to
keep it."

Tom reached out a finger to stroke the
cat's arched back and then decided not to
touch it after all. It looked too dangerous,
fizzing with anger.

"It's like my ice cat," he said. "That just grew out of the snow."

"Yes, I saw it," Dad said. "It reminded me, too. That's why I took this cat out of the drawer to show you."

He put the ice-green cat away in his pocket, as if he thought it might leap out of his hand and claw someone if he held it there any longer.

"That's a nasty cat," he said. "But there are other sorts of cat. I haven't done any carving for a while, but maybe the new drugs the doctor's given me will help. And then I shall make another cat – a friendly cat, the sort of cat that sits by the fire and purrs."

A spark of hope leaped up inside Tom.

"New drugs?" he said. "Are you going to be cured?"

"No, Tom. Not cured," Dad said. "I shall never be able to run about or carry heavy things or be really strong again. There will be good days and bad days, and yesterday was a bad day. But there are other things I can still do. I can go to work, and carve my animals, and read, and do a bit of cooking, and we can all go to the pictures and out for the day and on holiday. I can still be a dad. And now," Dad said, "I think it's time we went down and got some breakfast. And then you'd better go round to Gary's and say you're sorry."

Tom had forgotten about Gary. That wasn't going to be easy.

Chapter Five

After breakfast, he put on his boots and anorak and walked slowly round to Gary's front door. Gary's mum opened it, not looking at all pleased to see him.

"Gary's not coming out today," she told Tom. "He's busy upstairs."

Tom knew that she knew about the snowman, and that Gary knew too. Gary didn't even want to talk to him, so how was he supposed to say sorry?

It was a grey, dreary Sunday anyway, not

the sort of day that made Tom want to play outside. He went back in, and Dad helped him to mend his broken truck, and then all three of them – Mum, Dad and Tom – wrapped Christmas presents until lunch-time.

Next day was Monday and Tom was back at school. He tried to be nice to Gary, lending him his felt-tips and offering to work together for Maths, but Gary wasn't in a mood to be friendly. At break, when Tom tried to say he was sorry about the snow-

man, Gary would only shout at him: "You wrecked my snowman, on purpose! You're just jealous, that's what you are! Cos my snowman was tons better than your stupid cat." And then he ran off before Tom could say any more.

It started to snow again during afternoon school: big, soft flakes that settled on the playground and on the road outside. Lorries were out on the roads to spread grit, and the car tyres turned it all to black slush that sprayed over the legs of people walking on the pavement. But it was still snowing, and when Tom went home he saw that fresh snow had covered the ruins of the snowman and the ice cat. He looked up. The sky was like a thick grey blanket, with snowflakes spinning down so fast that they made him dizzy.

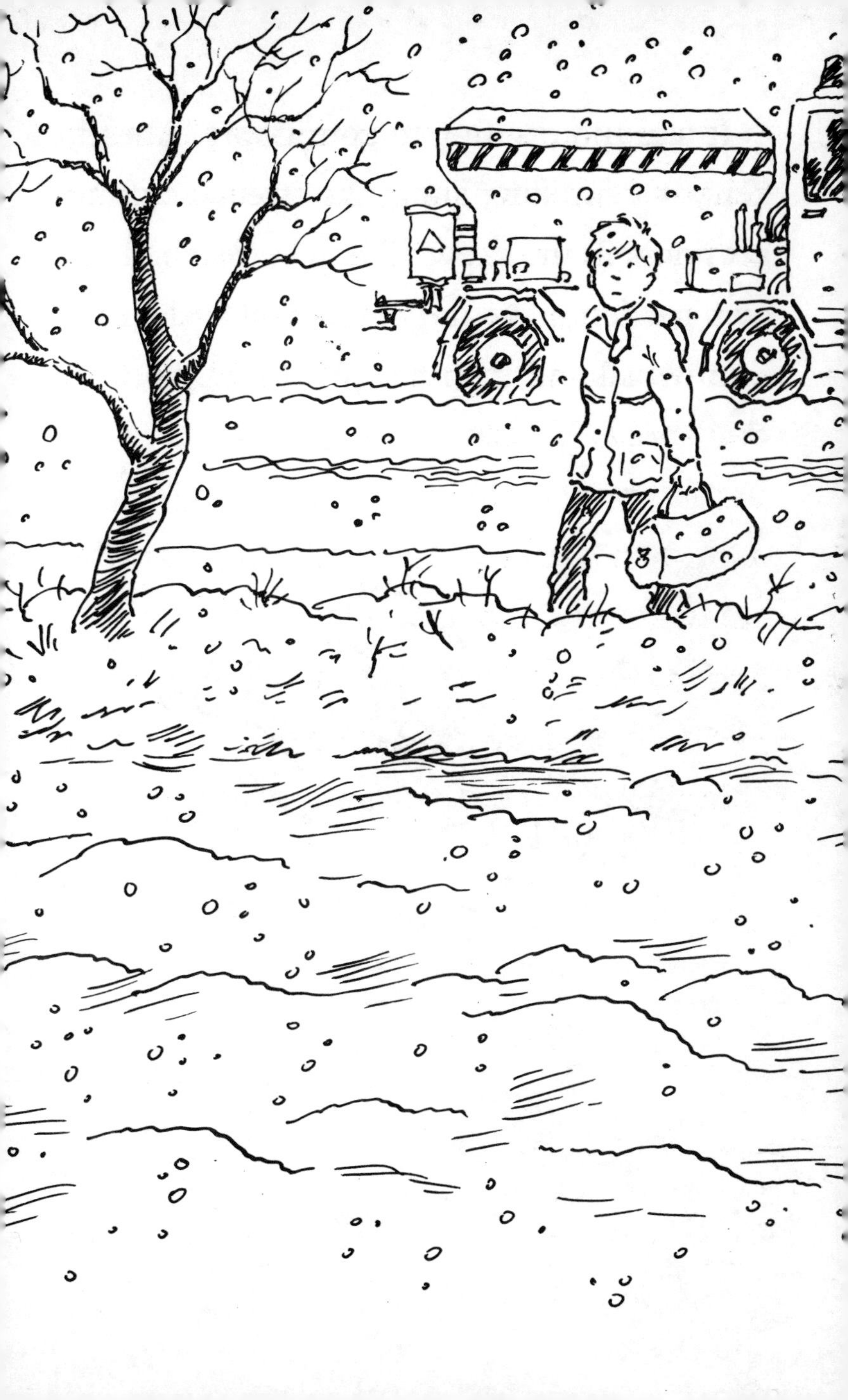

It was too exciting to go indoors. Ahead, Gary was walking along the street, scuffing his boots in the snow. When he reached his own garden he bent down to roll and shape a snowball and then he aimed it at Tom.

"Missed!" Tom aimed one back and it spattered on Gary's sleeve. "Hey, let's make a new snowman!" Tom shouted. "There's just about time before it gets dark."

"Okay!" Gary yelled back, forgetting to be cross. "A joint snowman, between your garden and mine."

They dumped their school bags and started, not trying to beat each other this time, but trying to beat the darkness. They filled their hands with snow, and carried and moulded and shaped and patted while the light dimmed to blue and the street lights flickered on.

"A snow*man*, you said," Gary panted. "This looks like turning into another cat."

"It can't be!" Tom scooped another double handful and moulded it in place. "The ice cat's gone away." It had gone for good; he knew that. He hadn't actually seen it go but he knew it had slunk away some time yesterday, and with its going the icy hardness inside him had melted away. He didn't want another ice cat.

"I don't mind," Gary said. "Anyone can make a snowman. This looks like turning out a pretty decent cat."

Tom looked at it. There it was – a big round cat like the one Dad had described.

Not a fierce ice cat; this one was a friendly cat that would like to curl up by the fire or drink milk from a saucer or just sit on your lap and be stroked. A cat with a flat sleek

body and a bushy tail curled round its front
paws.

"Did you mean to make that?" Gary said,
standing back.

"No," Tom said. "It just sort of grew."

It was a cat for Dad, the cat he wanted to
make for himself.

Tom looked towards the front window of the house and saw Dad standing there watching. Dad smiled, and just for a moment Tom thought the cat purred.

The End